"S" is for Smokescreen
Stories by Peter Best

Published by Peter R. Best

"S" is for Smokescreen. This is a work of fiction. Names, characters, places and incidents are all used in a fictitious manner.

Text copyright © 2014 by Peter R. Best

ISBN-13: 978-1495273957
ISBN-10: 1495273954

Dedicated to students in classrooms
1-4 of the
Robert B. Jolicoeur School

"Words can light fires in the minds of men.
Words can wring tears from the hardest
hearts."

-Patrick Rothfuss

Contents

Introductions

"**P**lease, I'm begging you; skip this part of the book."

Sometimes I feel like saying that when it comes to short books and short stories and prefaced introductions. I can't help but think that reading this part of the book is like studying how a coin trick works before seeing it performed. Or like buying the finest film ever made and deciding to watch the "behind-the-scenes" featurette first. Or perhaps opening a gift on Christmas day only to find yourself strangely preoccupied with wrapping paper. Comparisons abound. I guess at this point it's apparent that I'm just stalling in hopes that you'll get bored and skip past this section. My biggest issue with prefaces and introductions can be summed up in something my friend once said: "Introductions are for squares— they're boring." In some cases, I'm inclined to agree with him. Really—things don't quite get interesting until you flip to page 19. You should most likely do that now.

Have I convinced you yet? Have you found your way to the stories in this book—truths that exist only in a world obscured by a smokescreen of shadow and twilight—stories that could *almost* and *never*, be possible? Or are you still stuck in this world, still trying to find out how they're written? If you're still reading, that's alright, I suppose. There is yet a scenario or two in which you are not a complete square about to be bored out of your mind.

Like me, you might be engaged in the trade of word-smithing and tale-spinning. So for you, these introductions are helpful in that they expose the wiring underneath the words. That's fine in it's way, except that now I can't help compare you to an audience member at the unveiling of Thomas Edison's light bulb who asks to pull out the bulb's filament wire for inspection. Another comparison. I can't help myself when it comes to comparisons today.

The point I'm making is that whenever

you nail down the method behind a piece of magic—be it a coin trick, a light bulb or a story—you drive your nail into a coffin. The magic of writing only starts to come alive when you forget the mechanics of your prestidigitation and find sparks flying from your pen by rote. Sadly, the opposite is also true.

I'm not sure why so many collections and anthologies of fiction include space for introductions. It's possible that they are an attempt to appetize the reader with little tidbits before he or she dives into the main course of the book. It's probable that the writer just wants to brag a little. But it's certain that introductions are a part of tradition, and that's a part of why they are here. At the very least, they can elucidate the deeper concepts beyond the stories while still maintaining conventions of form. Some people's minds are built differently than mine, and for those people, seeing the filament wires before show time is part of the magic—maybe even most of the magic. If you're one of those people, then I really hope you do enjoy these little paragraphs of trivia. Without further ado, let's get the formalities over with, then get to the good stuff.

The Boy and the Astronaut

One night, I quite literally wrote a story in my sleep. I imagined a string of scenes built from pictures in my subconscious. I imagined a boy and an astronaut and other things, terrible and wonderful. When I woke up, I scrambled to my yellow-paper pad and jotted down the entire plot before it faded from my memory. I was about to write the finishing sentence when I looked up from my work and saw a penguin sitting on my desk. It was breathing shallowly and dusting snow off of its feet.

I woke up in earnest then, unable to believe my luck—two drafts of a story already completed, dreamed inside of each other like descending Russian dolls. Assuming that I have no more waking up to do, I now have a story about children, grownups, and the cost incurred when a wayward person refuses to be loved.

Rosewood Taylor

I wrote this story on the back of a coupon while I rode on a train from Florence, Italy to Rome. Like a lot of my writing, I didn't think about it while I wrote it—whenever I try to write something edgy or cool, the prose always ends up peppered with explosions and high-speed chases. So, I learned early on not to try hard at anything when I write. I do remember feeling very lonely on that train ride and I remember possessing a guitar that served as a welcome distraction from some of my struggles.

I never owned a Taylor G.S. 7, but the name just seemed like a natural choice and it helped me beg two questions: "How related can femininity and a crafted guitar really be?" and "Could an instrument ever function as a personified substitute for a soul mate?" The latter question is, as you'll find out, rhetorical. Beyond that, I hope this story will simply act as salve and solace to someone who feels the same way I did about loneliness, love and self-doubt.

The Last Historian

Ah, another story written during a bus ride! This piece was typed on a laptop, thankfully, somewhere between Lima and Huaraz, Peru. I had just read an article about *Theseus' Paradox* and was surprised to find how many incarnations the philosophical question had taken. The classic version goes something like this:

If you sailed in a boat, and you loved the boat so much that you replaced all of it's parts, plank by plank, would it be the same boat years later?

The question is a fun one and it's been used on a myriad of objects (a darned sock here; an axe with a replaced handle there) but it gets more serious if we apply it to ourselves. At what point of change do we cease to remain the same person? If indeed we traverse the themes of identity so as to follow this question to its end, we have to examine our physicality and spirituality in order to come to a satisfying conclusion.

The Last Historian provides no specific answer, but it does playfully toy with the question, and it does a whole lot of hinting all the while.

Wild Seeds

I'm not sure what I was going for when I wrote *Wild Seeds*. I know I wanted to capture something: perhaps the awkwardness of first encounters, perhaps the excitement and nervousness of a hormone-fraught teenage experience. Whether or not I was successful in capturing either of these things, the theme I grasped most completely in this cautionary tale was the way a young woman looks to a young man: alluring, dangerous, and alien. Perhaps more alien than you might initially believe.

The Grand, American Curtiss Aeromobile

The year before I graduated from college I decided to research early attempts that engineers had made at "aero-mobiles" as part of a project in a fiction workshop class. I sifted through various inventor biographies and I found one man particularly intriguing—a surly pioneer named Glenn Curtiss. From the small amount of information I had to draw upon, he stood out from other aviation pioneers because of his edgy attitude. Born at the turn of the 20th century, he engaged in the profession of aviation not to capitalize on the newborn motor industry, but because of his genuine love for driving and designing anything that could propel a man forward at neck-breaking speed. Before founding the Curtiss Aeroplane and Motor Company, he built his own one-cylinder motorcycle that utilized a tomato can for a carburetor and set a world land speed record of sixty-four miles per hour—just four years later, he more than doubled the speed of that record.

Another element of his character that solidified him as a consummate renegade was his insistence to not only design aero-mobiles, but to test pilot them as well. Curtiss possesses the characteristics of a dreamer and while his ideas didn't always have a practical space in the real world, he is one of the most innovative minds in early aeronautics. Surprisingly, the recognition credited to his life's work is very limited, and much of his life has not been chronicled. In part, this is why he is referred to in my story as "the unsung motorist."

Because of his daredevilry and relative obscurity, I felt that almost one hundred years later in 2014, it was appropriate for him to become a folk hero at last. This is to say that he was born long enough ago, and has enough room in his life to be filled in by fiction, for his character to lend itself to legend. To me, he embodied the pre-World War optimism, patriotism, and American pride that characterized the early 1900s. Though in actuality he passed away from an attack of appendicitis, the last scene of Glenn Curtiss' life described in this account seems more appropriate to who he was.

Six Months' Time

I really think you'll find that the first line of *Six Months' Time* says a lot. It's a science fiction piece, but barely science fiction. Our world is changing, and certain elements of this story will not remain science fiction for long. In 2014, we live in a time where fact sometimes extends into stranger realms than does fiction. For the first time, young adults without wrinkles or liver spots are scratching their heads and cursing an ever-changing stream of technology. I knew I had to write this story when I bought an external hard drive for my laptop. It was about the size of a large-print Bible; it stored a thousand gigabytes and it was the hottest thing on consumer shelves. Barely a couple of years later (or so it seemed) I found myself searching online for another hard drive, this time online. To my surprise there was one advertised that was no bigger than my pinky finger. It stored the same amount of space—a thousand gigabytes. *Six Months' Time* contains my predictions, my anxiety and my mixed feelings about our changing world.

Someone Else's Job

There was a time when I tried daily to force my mind into creative production. I didn't have a whole lot of fun back then because I didn't understand what ideas were or where they came from. While I still don't know either of those things, I know that good ideas aren't summoned from within. We can't just mold an idea into formation and work it into being. Ideas are more like fish that we're lucky enough to catch if our mental nets happen to be in the right place in the ocean, at the right time. Ideas are scary in a sense, because they can't really be controlled—they don't belong to us. So, it stands to reason that if a person truly did have the ability to create something as dangerous as an idea and furthermore, to bring that idea into reality, he would be in a very frightening predicament indeed.

Tower of Selfoss

The roads were iced over and the walkways were snowed in. The world was very quiet when I wrote *Tower of Selfoss* and life seemed to be very simple, if only on an external level. I decided to write a story more or less from a child's perspective. A story in which a nine-year-old could build a snow tower up into the sky—a story in which a child has to ask himself what it means to grieve and to search for something illusive. The challenge for me was to ask myself what it means to build a tower of accomplishments and to find what exists on the top tier. At the end of it all, I don't completely know what the story really means, but I know enough about myself to understand that it's a metaphor. When I find out what that metaphor means I'll be sure to let you know.

Sudoku and Reindeer Droppings

Once upon a time, Saint Nicholas lived and walked and breathed. He went by the title *Bishop* Nicholas and he looked more like an elf than a rotund giant. He lived in the Grecian town of Myra—not on the "North Pole" or beyond the mountains of

Korvatunturi. A blend of tradition and history asserts that he performed multiple acts of charity, that he worked his fair share of miracles, and that he participated in religious fasts even during childhood. He was described as a man with a short temper and a loving heart—contradictory drives that make his true character all the more interesting. Today, if you were to visit his tomb on the island of Gemile, you can witness orthodox priests who bottle a rose-scented liquid that miraculously streams from his grave.

But in the western world he's become something else entirely. He wears a silly cap and a red coat and he's always touching his finger to his nose. *Sudoku and Reindeer Droppings* deals with the problem of what happens to the real Saint Nicholas when society no longer has room for him. If nothing more, this story restores a bit of dignity to the ancient Saint: a dignity that's been long-neglected and much-deserved.

The Boy and the Astronaut

The boy shouted from deep in his chest while he rocketed up through the atmosphere, his jetpack spitting dragon's breath as he soared.

"Flight, freedom, and not even gravity to hold me down!"

He shot from the terrestrial gravity like a bullet through cotton and released the throttle on his flight apparatus as the sky winked from blue to black. His wild eyes swept across waves of nictitating stars that dotted a black ocean of space. He took in the panorama, searching for two specific luminous points. The boy had done this a thousand times; he was no stranger to the sapphire terrere below him, the surface of wisped white and robust brown, the dirty-gold glow of city lights and the occasional green and pink haze of an aurora borealis. From the corner of his eye, he spotted something white, grey and reflective. The figure was fitted with panels that shimmered in the sun's rays and, from where the boy hovered, it looked to be less than twenty kilometers away. A smirk sprouted across his lips and he aimed his thrusters, steering himself towards the station.

A timer ticked faithfully and a cheerful, pre-recorded female voice made an announcement inside of Commander James' space helmet.

"Fifty minutes of oxygen remaining."

Tick. Tock. Tick.

James clutched his shuttle tether with the crook of his elbow and removed a screwdriver from the fastening hook on his astronaut's glove. His shuttle's maintenance task was minutes from completion. He'd performed extra-vehicular duties in space a thousand times over the course of his captainship but even now, he couldn't say he'd completed a spacewalk without coming close to making a mess in his suit at least once. As he roped himself towards the vessel, he saw what looked like a piece of sizeable debris advancing quickly towards him. The astronaut's attention snapped into vigilance as the figure loomed. It was shaped like a boy. The figure wore no space suit, just tattered clothes and a jetpack. The boy was pale and looked like he hadn't eaten in a long while.

Deep breaths, James thought. *Call to mind your training.*

After all, it was nothing more than a space-induced hallucination. There was no use panicking—that would just use up oxygen. James would have to roll with the vision.

Let the dream run its course.

The astronaut couldn't call out to the boy (how could anyone hear him in space?) but, against logic, something made the old space explorer move a finger to his suit's external speaker switch.

Click.

"Ho, stranger! Welcome to the ATSS-398. You have full permission to approach and dock, should you so desire."

The boy beamed a coy grin and appeared to understand the astronaut.

"Ho," he said. His voice was indifferent.

From close range, Commander James saw a ratty green t-shirt on the boy. It had once displayed a logo but had deteriorated into a crumbling circle that reminded James of cracked desert clay. The boy's shorts were dress slacks, cut off at the knees. Deep holes were worn into the pant legs around the pockets.

"Would you like something to wear?" asked James kindly. "I can't imagine you could be very warm in your current attire."

The boy clutched the leather straps of his jetpack, bringing his arms in close to his tiny chest. For a long time he floated silently, observing the man with simple interest.

"*Forty minutes of oxygen remaining*," the voice announced.

Tick. Tock. Tick.

The boy said finally, "I need to find the North Star."

"Polaris?" asked James.

"The boy nodded. I'm trying to locate a point near the North Star."

"V603-Ursa is pretty close."

"No, not that star."

"Well, V641-Ursa Major, then." James twisted in a slow drift and grasped his tether tighter. He pointed his fastening hook to the twinkling fleck.

"Yes, the second star to the right of the North Star," said the boy.

The boy squinted and reignited his thrusters, facing away from the astronaut. He seemed ready to shove off until James heard a malicious giggle over the cylinder's roar.

"I know you," said the boy.

James shook his head, slowly. "I don't believe we've met."

"I am from London," said the boy. "I launched this jetpack out of Kensington Gardens."

"How nice," said James, and bit his tongue. The boy was a hallucination; hallucinations didn't need to be honest.

"I'm captain and commander of the ATSS-398. I call it the Jolly Roger. He motioned to a slightly crooked insignia stenciled onto the vessel's belly. The name's James. I'm from America, but I got my education in the UK. Eton and Balliol and all that. Lovely place, England. Rainy, but lovely."

The boy said nothing; just looked at

James with an air of juvenile self-importance that reminded him of his primary school peers.

"You know," said the Astronaut, after an awkward pause. "Perhaps you do remind me of someone after all."

The boy resembled a disheveled teenager who had vandalized the outside door to James' flat during his undergraduate days at Balliol. James had shrugged the matter off when an officer asked if he wanted to press charges. He sent the boy on his way home with a light scolding, not having the heart for punishment. The next day, the word "WANKER" had been drizzled in bright red spray paint across the outside of his bedroom window. *Lesson learned*, he had thought.

The boy's eyes darted from the man's face, to the captain's badge sewed to his shoulder, to the fastening hook screwed to his glove.

"And you," said the boy, "remind me of someone I used to know very well."

"Someone in your family?"

"No."

"One of your teachers, then."

"No. A man without a space shuttle. A man who kept a different kind of ship."

"*Thirty minutes of oxygen remaining,*" the voice counted down.

Tick. Tock. Tick.

James fidgeted in his suit and changed the subject. "May I ask where you're headed?

"Somewhere far, far away."

"And...how far is that?"

"I don't know. Four hundred, maybe five hundred light-years away. I should be there by morning if I make a straight trek."

The astronaut gaped. "Are you crazy?"

"Perhaps." The wicked grin re-lighted across the boy's visage.

"With all the fuel in that jetpack, you wont survive a hundred miles."

The boy's smile cracked for half a moment and James glimpsed an involuntary shudder that the boy tried to hide.

The boy jetted closer to the astronaut and James found himself clutching his tether with his full strength.

"I've survived a thousand summers

without so much as a year's toll on my back," jeered the boy.

James persisted, a tremor in his voice. "It's less than negative four hundred degrees out here. At least come aboard the vessel before you go. I have a trained crew inside that can provide you with food and a spare spacesuit."

The boy's knees began to shake, the knobby caps turning purple.

"Son, there are dangers in space. Things that *I'm* afraid of. Pressure and radiation, cosmic wavelengths and microscopic things that eat your flesh away in the dark." Closer, the boy flew, until the Captain could see the child's phantasmal breath frost on the glass of his helmet.

"But I'm not flesh, am I, Captain James?" The boy said after a pause. "And neither are you."

The astronaut just hovered stupidly, speechless and confused.

"We've known each other, Captain, on a thousand different levels, over a hundred different planes, in a dozen different worlds."

The boy doubled over suddenly and

hacked a retching cough as if rattled with croup.

"You're speaking rubbish," said James in a strangled whisper. "Come in from the cold and we'll make sense of this."

The boy regained himself and continued. "We are hopes and fears, you and I. Concepts and drives and only are we flesh and blood when we represent something larger than *us*. Burden and Flight: that is what we are. You are Responsibility and I am Freedom. You are the Captain and I am the crewmate who refuses to subordinate.

"*Twenty minutes of oxygen remaining*," the voice counted down.

Tick. Tock. Tick.

"This is a madman's tête-à-tête," said Captain James. "I'm no enemy. On the contrary, I'm offering shelter from the cold, from the dark. Could that be so bad?"

The boy pushed gently into the astronaut's tether.

"We've been battling since the dawn of history and it always ends the same way, old man."

"Stop this scandal at *once*," the astronaut stammered. You must know my intent is not to…to…keep you *captive*. I would never try to *harm* you."

"I know," said the boy, icily.

The Astronaut held out his free arm. "Then take my hand. I'll vow it: my intent is to *care* for you."

The boy's eyes darkened cruelly, as if remembering something.

"*That*, I will *never* allow."

Swifter than wind, the boy seized the fastening hook on James' glove and brought it down hard across the tether, severing it smartly from the space station.

He let out a crow then— a shrill, murderous cry— and turned away, rocketing towards a broad pan of stars that grew viciously brilliant.

James could hear the boy shouting a mantra into the distant void. "Freedom, flight, and not even gravity to hold me down!"

The astronaut, anxious and bewildered, slipped languidly into the eternal night. Light crept from his eyes and his limbs went numb. The last thing he heard before

———

space swallowed him like the jaws of a leviathan crocodile was a cheery female voice.

It announced, *"Ten minutes of oxygen remaining,"* followed by a gentle and steady countdown.

Tick. Tock. Tick.

Rosewood Taylor

Eric Grant was not a lover, but he understood the nature of love.

Eric had never had a girlfriend, or a sweetheart, or even a valentine, but he did possess a Taylor G.S. 7 acoustic guitar that he took wonderful care of and played every night without fail. Eric was not a lover, but if there was one thing that Eric Grant was built to do, it was to love.

Eric often admired the design of his acoustic Taylor and felt that the curvaceous make of the instrument lent it a uniquely feminine quality. It was all arches and swirls and underneath the fine-spun spruce surface, it was elegant, though not *delicate* as its exterior suggested. Eric understood his Taylor well. He knew the right flourishes and hammer-ons for his fingers to press and what strings to massage; he knew to listen to the sounds his Taylor made and to adjust his technique accordingly; he knew to throw his heart into the rhythm— it was his only hope— and he knew that in the purest moments of his music, he filled the same space in the world as did his Taylor.

Eric Grant had never been a lover. He was quiet among others and shy around women and this had started when he was in middle school. Eric was walking outside on the last day of the school term, when Ian Raimi, a boy who had been held back a year, kicked his legs out from under him and two of Ian's friends jabbed at Eric's side. They prodded at him as he scrambled to his feet and kicked him in the testicles. He stood his ground well for a boy of his age, but he could not keep his eyes from welling and the group of boys called him a faggot when they saw him on the verge of tears. This sort of thing repeated itself until Eric was enrolled in high school and had developed certain beliefs about himself.

By then, something had melted, or snapped, or dissolved, or crumbled inside of him. What Eric endured didn't crush his spirit, but it did form a crack inside of him, a crack that would grow into a fissure, a fissure that would become a wide divide between himself and the people around him.

In his school years he felt certain of little, but when his fingers brushed the cool rosewood neck of his Taylor, he knew what to do. He knew what notes to leave open and he knew what chords to barre; he knew when to push his palm firmly against the guitar's mahogany backing and he knew when to pull back with all the pliancy of which he was capable; he knew when the time was right for him to let loose a pattern of close-grained percussive strumming and he sensed in advance the moments for slow, steady finger picking.

Eric Grant would never be a lover and on some level, he knew this. He grasped the phenomenon of love thoroughly enough to know that it was not something that was simply given, but something that must also be received. This was something Eric did not know how to do— not while he believed he had nothing worthwhile to offer in return.

But, he did know how to sweep his pick against fine steel strings and he knew how to gently mute his Taylor's vibrations with his palms; he knew how to arpeggiate the highest and sweetest notes and make them hang in the air after they were born from his Taylor's cedar box chamber; he knew how to tease out culminating intervals on his Taylor's rosewood fret board and he knew how to follow the scales, spiraling his hands furiously higher, until the sounds his guitar made were the deep groans akin to those of a bass.

Eric was not, had never been, would never be a lover.

So, he waited until he was old and he hoped until he was bitter and his fingers clung, lovingly, to a hollow wooden box.

The Last Historian

The old man looked blankly up from the operating table as the colony surgeon applied a scalpel to his ancient cranium, incised through the top layer of his scalp and cut a neat, three-inch patch of flesh away. The skin was peeled back and a surgical saw began to buzz. The man heard a pitchy hum, followed by a deep grind as the saw bore into his bare, milky-pink skull. He sighed. This was nothing new.

"If the handle on that saw were to break,

would you replace it?" he asked.

"The colony surgeon paused from his work. "Of course I would. Wouldn't be much use to me otherwise."

The scent of burnt marrow was in the air. The old man scrunched one side of his nose. "And if the blade eventually cracked, what would you do then?"

The colony surgeon inched a pair of clamps into the incision and extricated the patch of bone. The man's ancient brain was clearly visible now, stitch-marks winding like road lines across the bumpy grey terrain.

"Replace it, of course. But nothing's going to go wrong with the blade. Now, don't tell me you've got nerves about the replacement surgery."

The man laughed. "How could I? Almost all my nerves are mechanical. Synthetic adrenalin is more sophisticated than that."

The surgeon turned and opened the door to a refrigerator and pulled out what looked like a lunchbox with a biohazard sticker slapped on the side."

I suppose I was just wondering, if you

were to replace the handle to that saw, would it be the same saw it was, before it broke?" Blood dribbled from the opening in the man's head and the surgeon dabbed at it with a sterile cloth.

"Absolutely, it would be the same." The surgeon looked puzzled.

"And if you replaced the blade as well?"

"Same saw, pretty much," the surgeon replied, automatically.

"Now, suppose you were so sentimental about that saw that you replaced not only the handle and the blade, but the nuts and bolts also and even the copper wiring in the cord. What then?"

The surgeon opened the box on the table and a haze of cold steam rose to his face. Inside the box was a grey two-inch organ that reminded him of a large slug.

"I don't understand where you're going with this question," he said to the man. "I guess that's why I'm the colony surgeon— not the colony philosopher. Perhaps after we transplant this new broca's organ into your brain, you can ask me the question again."

"*My* brain," mused the man.

"Interesting."

"After all, you're speech patterns have deteriorated in the last few decades. I'd bet it will be easier to express yourself after the graft."

The man looked sadly into the surgeon's eyes. "They say a person's speech is often the last thing to go."

"Don't worry. That will all be fixed once we replace the old organ with the new. Think of the procedure as if we're darning a pesky hole in your favorite pair of socks."

The man nodded, wondering if he looked as scared as he felt. He knew what the surgeon would tell him, that this procedure was the same as the last hundred procedures; simple maintenance, that was all. He remembered clear as day how the surgeon had looked as a shy boy of seven; how he had looked on the day he was born. And now the boy who had grown into a surgeon was telling him not to worry, as if reassuring a child.

The surgeon squeezed a tiny hydraulic attached to a long needle, and a thin rope of clear fluid spurted from the shaft.

"One last question, doctor," whispered

the man. "What will happen to the original organ?"

"Same as all the other parts. I'll put it in storage if I can, depending on the organ's state of quality. Or it might be sent to the Academy for research. We don't have to dispose of it, if that's what you're getting at. The surgeon picked up a smaller scalpel, this one serrated and hooked at the end. "Although I've never known you to be sentimental about, uh, *old parts*.

A needle drew deep into the man's brain and he could no longer speak as the language center of his brain was first neutralized, then removed. The man had undergone a million grafts, a million transplants. The wrinkled and mismatched quilts of his skin carried surgical marks that rested upon older scars, ones that had all but faded from sight and memory. Fingers and toes and limbs and hearts and brain tissue all transplanted a hundred times over on the man. It was expensive, but his particular line of work made the medical procedures a necessity over the millennia of his employment. And the man wasn't exactly indispensable. He was the only person in his particular line of work.

They called him the Historian. He watched the people of the final colony and he recorded what he saw. He saw men in straw hats plowing the fields; saw women gathering fruit from the orchards. He saw boys in denim trousers and girls in long dresses playing under the cold, red sun, and he wrote it all down. He was the only one who recorded the past, because the Elders knew what would happen if more than one Historian kept their own records. First, these subjective stories would differ, and then they would contradict. Discord would spring from contradiction and war would spring from discord. This had all happened eons ago in a time as detached from the colony as the dimming stars in the sky. He was the only Historian, and so he would have to live forever.

His eyes saw other things too, but he made sure never to record them: memories and thoughts and emotions of the donors who had replaced his older parts. These flashed into him and clung to his being like phantom limbs. The more he watched and recorded and remembered the people around him, the more he seemed to forget of himself. He had a name once, before the Elders chose him. Was it Gideon? He thought that was his name, but other times he couldn't help but feel it had once been Carlos. During fractured moments of clarity, he could almost remember those eons ago when he had been a citizen, no replacements, no synthetics. He could all but swear there had been days where he had run and jumped and farmed and played and kissed and procreated. Those days seemed as though they were lived by someone else, and in so many ways, they were.

In recent centuries, he'd felt sparks and currents crackling through his frame, as machine parts replaced more and more of his anatomy. In recent decades, he had closed his eyes and on occasion found himself dreaming in zeros and ones. Fewer and fewer organic donors were available to him now; the colony was shrinking. After all, the Elders called it the final colony.

The Broca's organ had been the only part left which he'd been born with, and now that was gone too. He remembered this as he awoke and pulled himself upright.

The Historian circled a fingertip along his fresh stitches, then pulled the needles and tubes from his various veins. He tied his hospital gown and brought a chair to the room's window.

Boys and girls were still playing outside in the long, brown-green grass. Men and women were still working in the fields. The weather was cold and the sun was as red as it ever had been at mid-day. He pulled a chair from the corner of the room and sat in it, shivering from the coldness that seeped through the cracks in the hospital window.

The man had once observed a young couple fighting outside in the hospital courtyard. He caught only a snippet of the quarrel, and he recorded it.

"I mean, we're not getting any younger," the woman had said to her husband. "Our lives are passing us by."

They had both died over a thousand years ago. The Historian had thought those words would never apply to him, but maybe he had been wrong. Had life passed him by? Had death? Perhaps after this last surgery, the man had finally died without even realizing it. Perhaps he had just been born. The man felt no different, save for an overwhelming numbness, possibly brought on by the antithetic the doctor had injected. For a long time he just sat, wondering whether he was a sock with a darned hole, or a surgical saw with its blade and handle replaced.

A metal door whushed open and the man heard the colony surgeon approach his chair by the window.

"Well, well," said the doctor. "Looks like you're feeling better. How's your speech?"

The man opened his mouth, but did not speak. He stood up from his chair, looking the doctor in the eyes. He saw so much in those eyes. He saw joy and discovery and anger. He saw compassion and failure and surprise.

He saw impatience and faith and suspicion and awe; saw cowardice and love and hope and sacrifice. He saw curiosity, fear, excitement and frustration, and he knew he no longer had a part in the things he saw. In a couple hundred years, none of those things would exist as more than written memories.

The Historian pushed past the colony surgeon and rushed through the metal doors, not bothering to collect his clothing. He sprinted out of the hospital and across the courtyard, the flaps of his gown trailing behind him. Out through the orchard he ran as the sun's color cooled from a ruby to a brick. Out past the wide fields of wheat and barley with stocks that had began to frost in the evening chill.

Finally, he crested the mountains that sheltered our colony and looked for all to see as though he had run over the edge of the world.

That was seventy years ago and many things have happened since. I do my best to record the events of the final colony where the last historian left off. I was just a boy then, but now I am one of the final colony's only senior citizens. Now my blood runs through my veins like molasses. Now I have arthritis in my lower back, wrists and fingers.

In particular, my fingers now resemble gnarled claws. The Elders have assured me there is a fix for my pain. They elected for me to undergo my first replacement surgery tomorrow. They have told me to rest from my duties. They assure me I will soon be able to scribe using a keyboard or pen again. They assure me that soon I'll feel more like my *old self.*

It is strange, sitting at this hospital window, waiting for the colony surgeon to arrive, seeing so much and being able to record nothing. Until the operation, I'll have to content myself in simply watching the sun dim as I wait to record what the Elders assure me will be a bright future for our colony.

Wild Seeds

"**S**ister, is the door open?"

"It is open, my sister, and the gate is unlocked."

"I've missed you so much."

"And I have missed you, my sister. It seems like eons you've been gone and now you are fully grown."

"Yes, Sister, I am called Violet now."

"A new name for a new home."

"It does not feel like home, Sister. The sun shines less than half of the day here. The nourishment is short, but it is raining tonight. It only rains here every few weeks."

The girl did not appear to be near a door or a gate. She placed her fingertips onto a rain-spattered bedroom window and kept them there, as if savouring the window's coolness. The frame was tressed with the kind of little green mood-bulbs you would expect to find in a college freshman's apartment and they cast a curious sheen across her skin.

Her eyes were large and her body swelled in curves, starting with her breasts, pinching in almost cartoonishly at her waist and bulging again at her fertile hips. She looked unnatural. Almost photo-edited. Almost not human.

"How are your children, Sister?" the girl asked.

"Fully raised and blown to the wind. I wish you could've met them. Soon they'll be sowing their own wild seeds, I suppose. And speaking of wild seeds— "

The girl pursed her lips in an attempt to keep from smiling.

"Yes, Sister, I've met a boy."

"I can *always* tell when you've met a boy, my sister."

"Yes, you always can. I am waiting for him. He has said he will visit me tonight."

It was the kind of night when dark clouds replaced the moon's presence in the sky. When even the shine of street lamps were muffled and if you were to drive an automobile, you would find your vision losing sight of the road lines and your headlights dampened. It was the kind of night where if it weren't for the urban streaks of red and yellow light across the wet black top, you would wonder whether or not you had slipped altogether into darkness.

Eamon stopped into the convenience store one block from Violet's apartment. He was late in meeting her, but wasn't sure if this was necessarily a bad thing. Did college girls care if you were especially punctual? He wiped a wet mop of hair from his eyes, wondering if there might be an effortless charm to being marginally late. He ducked into the store's *Snacks and Drinks* aisle and found an eighteen-ounce bottle of ginger ale.

"You bring the ginger. Let me worry about the whiskey," Violet had said.

Eamon was two years away from his high school graduation. He had never tasted alcohol, let alone a ginger and whisky. But, like college students, like Violet, like the opposite sex at large, it promised to be something exotic, if slightly dangerous, and it made him curious. He picked up the ginger ale and walked to the *Health and Grooming* aisle, where he slipped something into his back pocket that he was too embarrassed to purchase outright.

Just incase nature runs it's course tonight, he told himself.

When he first met Violet by the greenhouses at the community college, he posed the only question he could think to ask.

"Is gardening a hobby of yours?"

The girl brushed a lock of strawberry-blonde hair behind her ear, leaving a trace of soil in it. "I'm a botany major," she said. "But I took up gardening for my own...personal growth."

Eamon couldn't remember the things he said to her after that, but he would never forget the last question she had asked him.

"Would you like to see me again, Eamon?"

The spoken rhythm of that last sentence ricocheted happily through his head as he checked a scrap of paper with Violet's apartment number on it and climbed the steps to her lobby, three at a time.

"Tell me about your journey, my sister."

The girl considered for a moment. "It was aimless, but not long. No longer than it would take for a kernel to grow into a Pendunculate oak tree, to drop an acorn, and to watch it sprout into a sapling."

"Not very long at all then."

"Long or short, have you ever known a member of our family to be impatient, Sister?"

"A wise answer, my sister. Are there rainforests in your new home?"

"Just forests made of dead things. Of steel, concrete and glass."

"So, this new home is a rainforest without hope?"

"Not without hope, Sister," said the girl. "After all, it only takes one seed and a patch of willing soil to crack through a mile of gravel."

Eamon was shivering by the time someone answered the door, and it was not the girl he was expecting.

"You must be Violet's friend," said a tall, tanned girl with bangs straight enough to double as a ruler. She beckoned him inside and he followed her up a floor of stairs.

"Yes, thank you. I'm Eamon. And you must be a friend of Violet's?"

"I guess. She's uh, my roommate anyways." The girl closed the door behind Eamon and headed over to a bathroom mirror, where she resumed applying eyeliner. She left the bathroom door ajar.

Eamon put his ginger ale on the kitchen table and eyed his surroundings. "The two of you sure keep a lot of plants. It's like a *jungle* in here."

The girl rolled her eyes, then faced away from Eamon and pulled her top off, revealing a bright-pink bra strap banded along her upper back. "Well, Violet keeps them," she said over her shoulder, as she slid into a shiny blue blouse. "They give me the creeps, honestly."

She dabbed at her cheeks with a brush and motioned to a closed door that Eamon assumed led to Violet's room. A blue-white light that reminded him of a tanning bed shone from the bottom crack of the door. Eamon detected a conversation just out of discernable earshot.

"She's...on the phone, or something. Bad idea to interrupt her though, in my experience." The girl picked up a spray bottle and spritzed a light, sticky mist into her hair.

Eamon swallowed and took off his jacket. "Thanks for the tip."

"Don't sweat it, kid," she said, standing. "You can tell Violet I'll be out for the night. Don't get too wild while I'm gone."

As Violet's roommate slipped on a pair of heels and walked from the room, Eamon took a few steps toward the door. The blue-white light underneath the door crack seemed brighter now and the conversation grew clearer as he inched closer.

"It is cramped here, Sister."
"In the new sphere that you speak of?"
"In my new form. Imagine the miles of

your spindles huddled into a chamber just five feet long. I hope that when you arrive, you will not have to take such a form."

"Perhaps when my children and their children arrive, your tendrils will already be stretched across the planet."

"Indeed, Sister! And I have chosen the perfect mate to help me begin the process. He is tender, vernal, in the flower of his youth."

"And is he enamoured, my sister?"

"He has smelt my pollen, I will offer my nectar, and he will give me a seed."

"My beloved Sister, tonight you will cross-pollinate for the first time."

"Tonight, I will initiate the germination over my new planet."

There was a tap at the door and the girl wished her sister a hushed goodbye. Eamon stood on the other side of the door, his face confused in the lustre of green LEDs and sun lamps. His expression gave way to an eager grin when she stood and he saw the arches of Violet's figure thinly concealed under her lilac-patterned sundress.

"I heard that you needed to finish a phone call before I could see you," he said, as if already the knowledge had become hazy.

"Oh?" Violet remarked. "And how did you hear that?"

"Through the grapevine," he said. "Are you hungry?"

"*Starving.*"

Eamon glanced at a Venus flytrap on Violet's desk. "Um. Did you also want to catch a movie tonight, since we're already going out for food?"

The girl eyed him over and smiled teasingly. "Perhaps, that would be nice," she said. "But I think I'd rather spend a little more time indoors, first."

Eamon touched his back pocket, finding it strangely empty. Hadn't he slipped something important inside? Before he had a chance to retrospect any further, Violet had already pulled him onto her bed, and before he knew it, her body was on top of his and she was curling her arms snugly around him under the emerald light, twining her long fingers tightly into the spaces between his own.

The Grand, American Curtis Aero-Mobile

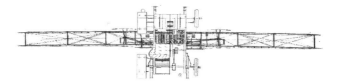

In the weathered clippings of
an antiquated newspaper, edges frayed and
pages stained, lingers the memory of the
most peculiar man that history has by and
large forgotten. As we survey his
abnormally lanky stature, captured grain by
grain in this early autochrome lumière
photograph, we can't help but imagine his

wild pride at setting the world land-speed record on a motorcycle of 136.36 miles per hour. We may choose to notice the pure, American ambition in his eyes, as we turn our own eye to the tattered grey image of one Mr. Glenn Curtiss, frowning deeply in concentration, wrinkling his bushy moustache into a nearly perfect semi-circle, on the day he would earn his first pilot license. A worn caption under his picture reads, "The Legendary June-Bug Flight: 1909".

Perhaps we'll even decide to pore over a photo-capture of the only day he would ever wear clothing as dandy as a tuxedo. Blinking the light out of our eyes as the camera-bulb sparks, sizzles and goes dark, we all but feel this curious man's bliss. Here, we witness what he considered his life's earliest and greatest accomplishment—an enduring marriage to his great love: Lena Pearl Neff.

And yet, we'll investigate none of these singular episodes, because, to tell the truth, we've only been summoned as silent witnesses to one historic and undocumented moment in Glenn Curtiss' short life. The day is bright and hot. Our hero dawns his apple cap and flight goggles and surveys in broad daylight his well-concealed invention that is soon to change the world. He smirks in spite of the fear that rides shotgun inside all men who risk their lives in the name of science. The man hoists his disproportionate, lanky frame onto the bicycle seat of the first flying automobile history has seen.

Upon the dashboard, conveniently doubling as the vehicle's central engine, rests the daguerreotype likeness of his wife. His eyes linger fondly on Mrs. Curtiss for a moment, then review two out-of-place pictures tucked and pasted into the heart of his flying car: the first of a blonde, balding man with cold eyes; the second, a picture of two brothers, Orville and Wilbur. His heart beating at a brisk staccato, Curtiss yanks the ripcord on his flight mobile and grips his patented handlebar throttle control. Like a mythical beast comprised entirely of gauges and dials, the Curtiss Aero-Mobile springs to life, at once gasping a thousand puttering breaths.

We must now zip along this dusty

runway to take in the complexity of the unsung motorist's contraption, unweildingly firing across the hot earth at a brisk fifty-eight. With a propeller mounted over each of the seven spinning wheels, four spanning wings (which perpetually flap like a tired pelican in migration) and an extravagant bat-like fin jutting out at the vehicle's front, one wonders whether some of Curtiss' gadgetry has any practical application. Foolish Glenn Curtiss! Do you believe the gaudy design of your life's project will help you when you have left the earth to rub shoulders with Gods? Aside from your observers, of whom you cannot possibly be aware, whom could this grandiose display intend to impress?

With gears and registers turning, shrieking, louder in his mind than the multiple roaring engines of the Curtiss Aero-Mobile, his eyes flicker again to the pictures on the dashboard engine. Glancing at the two Wright brothers who had sued him for patent infringement (and won) he envisions the sorry look soon to fall across their faces when his revolutionary invention will change the world. Next, he stabs a malicious fantasy towards the blonde and balding man, Henry Ford.

Perhaps the cut-throat bastard will bury his head under a rock when he realizes how trifling his inventions will be compared to this, he ponders loftily.

Upon his wife he simply gazes adoringly, mouthing, "I love you, sugar plum."

At last, his moment has arrived. A slipstream of air currents over the contraption's bottom wings, Bernoulli's principle is applied and the air pressure underneath the Aero-Mobile's metallic wings rockets Curtiss into the troposphere. At the exact moment that our modern Icarus ascends into a world of cumulus clouds, three things happen at once. A worker in a New Jersey based propeller factory congratulates himself on a scrupulous week's work; a scrap-metal craftsman counts his revenue and snickers at pawning off low-quality steel to a secretive inventor; a motor engineer from Hammondsport, Washington lies awake wondering whether the engine's hammering coil was supposed to have twenty-one or twenty-three serrated nodes.

The scheming mind of Glenn Curtiss no longer holds sway to the fantastic scene which we behold, but is preoccupied in the distant future of the 1950s, in which each and every family will ride into town in their own Curtiss Aero-Mobile.

"Should we take the thoroughfare or the airway to visit Grandma?" he pictures one child eagerly asking his mother.

"If it wasn't for that *genius* Glenn Curtiss, we wouldn't be able to take *either* route," replies the child's mother, shaking her head in reverent appreciation.

Glenn's self-indulgent fantasy is interrupted by a sickening lurch, followed by a throaty groan from deep in the belly of his engine. The whirring of the engine speeds faster, faster still, until acrid smoke spews out of its every orifice. The first car ever to take to the skies begins a return to its native earth with such speed that two wings of thin sheet metal are torn completely away. The propellers spin faithfully, but they alone are not enough to keep Curtiss airborne.

Frantically tweaking each lever and

pulley, Curtiss tries in vain to establish a state of balance in the heavens. As he plummets, the palm-sized likeness of his beloved Lena Pearl flaps violently and is whisked away by a gust of air, bereaving him of any company save Ford and the Wright brothers staring him sternly in the face. His fear rising, his vehicle tumbling, the wax in Curtiss' fabled wings begins to melt in earnest. Wind whistles through his goggles and he glimpses through blurry eyes the landscape becoming lucid, like a brown and green patchwork quilt coming into focus.

We must now leave Curtiss here in his darkest hour, as he plunges entirely from our sight and off the charts of recorded history. Because the complete remains of Curtiss and his Aero-Mobile were never found, speculation about his fate is controversial. There is one propeller manufacturer in New Jersey who believes Glenn Curtiss may well have survived the descent. Another party, this time a motor engineer in Hammondsport, Washington sent an interesting telegram that insisted:

"THE ENGINE WOULD HAVE PURRED BACK TO LIFE MOMENTS AFTER STOPPING*STOP*BUT THE AEROMOBILE COULD NEVER SUSTAIN SUCH A NOSEDIVE*STOP*."

Even one sheepish scrap-metal craftsman has commented on the matter, if only to stammer repeatedly that Curtiss' vehicle was made of the *finest* metal alloys.

Just one woman by the name of Lena Pearl remains curiously optimistic about the whole affair, defending the notion that Curtiss' dash alone may have been enough to pull him through his perilous experiment. When interviewed about her husband's ill fortune, she replies slyly that her Glenn just may be kicking around after all, working furtively in some secret corner of the earth, on an invention that will revolutionize the way of American life forever.

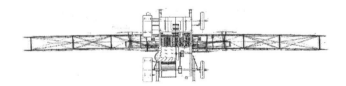

Six Months' Time

This is a science fiction story.
Kind of. But it won't be science fiction in
six months' time. No, in half a year it will
be pretty humdrum. Just wait and see, like I
did. In a year, by the time the Earth drags
itself around our antiquated sun, this story
will be obsolete, maybe fashionably so, if
I'm lucky. Staying power for maybe
another six months after that.

Have you ever heard of the term, *exponential growth*? It's hard to describe, but if you wanted, I could upload a neural-to-visual representation of the concept to my phone, or to my spectacles display, or my tablet or wallet screen. *Exponential growth* makes up a big part of the world these days, and when I was a boy, my grandfather described it with a story.

"A long time ago," I remember him saying, "In an age of famine, a starving Vizier endowed an honest Indian king with a ravishing hand-made chessboard." My grandfather settled into his armchair and unfolded his hands, sorting his mail. "When the astonished king asked how he might repay the generosity of his trusted official, the Vizier just smiled humbly, touched his stomach, and said, 'I ask only for a bit of rice to eat, placed on the chessboard in a doubling pattern: one grain of rice on the first square, two grains on the second square, four grains on the third, eight on the fourth, and so on.' The king swore it would be delivered and sent immediately for the rice."

My grandfather found his paycheck amid his heap of letters and ran his finger through the envelope, ripping the paper. I looked up from my handheld Game Boy.

"Anyways— you still listening?— the king doubled the rice away, but grew anxious once he portioned the rice for the fifth square: already it required *two-hundred fifty-six* grains. The king despaired once he reached the twenty-first square, for it demanded over a million rice grains, and once he reached the forty-second square, he was forced into disgrace and admitted to the Vizier that the world did not contain enough rice to fulfill his promise."

I paused my Game Boy for the second time and looked up at my grandfather. "You know, if that king had a computer, it would've been easy to figure out that he couldn't keep his promise. He would never have had to be embarrassed."

"Computers," scoffed my grandfather. "Never touch the techie-traps. They do more harm than good."

"What about Game Boys?" I asked. "You bought me this Game Boy for

Christmas."

He shrugged. "Play it all you want, just don't ask me to figure out how it works. *Nothing* is allowed to be simple anymore. Toys need directions, computers have some kind of code written under their caps, even— look!— even my paycheck has to be deposited electronically into my bank. No more hard cash, like the good old days."

I rolled my eyes.

"Go back to your game if you want," he said. "But mark my words: by the time you're my age, all your tech-junk is going to be for the worse."

I had a feeling he was wrong, but I didn't have plans to say, "I told you so."

"All the cyber-crap is piling up in this world," he finished with a wave of his hand, "The growth is going to be *exponential*."

What did the old curmudgeon really know, anyways? Game Boys and televisions and computers were awesome. Already, I didn't know how I could live without them. I just wished Bill Gates and Steve Jobs and the Nintendo wizards would pick up the pace a little. After all, I'd been playing a black-and-white Game Boy for two years now.

I didn't start to notice *exponential growth* until maybe seven or eight years later, but for all I know, the same technology curve had been curling upwards since the abacus, the drafting compass, the slide stick. Even later, I would look down at my cassette case, my portable CD player, my iPod, and wish I wouldn't have to wait so long for the cutting-edge stuff to hit the markets. But they hit sooner than I thought they would.

Nowadays, I just wish I could walk into a clothing store and buy a sweatshirt or hat without device-compatible wires sewn into the fabric. I wish I could buy a pair of prescription eyeglasses without embedded holographic display and built-in Wi-Fi for complementary web surfing.

First, the computers got smarter, then they got smaller, got shinier. They lost their keyboards and acquired touch-screens— very nice, *very* state of the art. Three-lettered tech-terms were born, evolved, were replaced, and died before there was time to memorize them: VHS to DVD to AVI stored on USB, but those quickly became so—last—month. Touch-screen tablets shrunk into all-purpose phones, and things didn't *really* start getting strange until after screen displays became bendable, portable, cheaper to produce than penny candy. Like a plague of locusts, the screens seemed to multiply and spread to every unravished surface of daily life. Screens with in-laid holographic displays plastered themselves to every wall, desk, fridge, ceiling and coffee mug. Once, I visited a hardware store to find that the only windows for sale were alternating opaque-translucent LCD windows.

As the years wore on, I had a recurring dream in which I saw a child version of myself playing video games at my grandfather's old house. The younger me always looked up from his Game Boy, pressed pause and said, "This is the world you always wanted, isn't it? One where you don't have to wait for the cutting-edge?"

Nowadays, when I wake up from those dreams, I just wish I could drag a stick of solid graphite across real paper instead of poking a stylus on a screen. I wish I could read a non-electronic newspaper without the breaking news pinging in and out of the front page; without headlines of electronic ink scrolling along each leaflet, slipping away from me, like the rest of the world.

"This is the *now*," a friend told me some time later. "Sustainable or not, you'd better stay current."

I scoffed. *A march to destruction, and I can't even keep up.*

My friend's advice was easier said than done. Last year, I traveled to Africa for a month-long service project. I returned with a cut on my hand to discover that robots were primarily responsible for precision surgery and dental work. When did that happen? Later on I read that a 3D printer had successfully built a functioning human heart. When 3D printing first became common, cardiologists predicted it would take thirty years to print human organs. Nano-technology meshed into twenty-five percent of consumer products and it wasn't long until electronic implants became popular: flexi-screens on our palms and speaker-receiver combos sewn in our fingertips. Sub-retinal display rooting became mostly affordable and even thought-controlled prosthetics for elderly folks didn't take long to develop.

Whatever you need. That was the motto. There were answers for everything: over satellite, across the web, through the wiki, on the Wi-Fi. There were programs to solve our present problems and newer programs to solve the problems caused by our program-derived solutions. *Exponential growth* continued to creep onwards and upwards. Our computers were getting smart, getting savvy, getting sarcastic even. And despite myself, I couldn't help but feel anxious about it.

Last week, I protested having a monitor chip surgically planted into my upper spine after my annual physical.

"Don't be *silly*," said a man-shaped android with a voice all too human. "The chip just monitors your vitals. We've known all your personal information for *years* now."

After I gave up and let the machines sew the chip into me, I rubbed the band-aid on my upper back and left the hospital. I stepped into my satellite-driven car and closed aging, tired eyes that had seen more than a lifetime of change. Now, I just wished I could go to sleep without a voice in my head asking if I wanted my dreams recorded. I wished I could walk down a street on a sunny day without a barrage of neuro-ads feeding directly into my brain.

My car began to drive and eventually grooved onto a back road that I didn't know. When it ground to a halt I was at my grandfather's house. He stepped onto his porch and waved his cane at me, smiling. Yes, he's still alive. And no, I'm not even close to the same age as my grandfather, even after everything that's happened. I'm twenty-six years old, but these days, a lot changes in a couple decades. I stepped into his living room and he pulled over a seat for me next to his armchair. He poured me some coffee and we sat talking, face-to-face. No instant message, no vid-chat equipment, just old-fashioned conversation. It had been a while since we did this, since anyone did this.

We talked about the new trends in space tourism and the accelerated probe to Alpha Centauri's closest exoplanet. We talked about the conflict between the Lunar and Martian colonies and all of the politics that the burgeoning civilizations were causing down here on Earth. I took an uneasy sip of coffee and spied an old Game Boy on my grandfather's coffee table. The old man unfolded his hands, picked up the Game Boy and flicked the screen to life. "Well, on the bright side," he said, "at least not *all* this tech-junk is for the worse. This Tetris game is actually pretty good."

"Well, I didn't have plans to say I told you so, Grandpa." I swallowed my coffee and then spoke before I knew what I was saying. "I guess…it just seems like *nothing* is allowed to be simple anymore."

He nodded. "All the shiny toys you can imagine, but nothing to remind you you're alive. It kind of reminds me of a story about a far away king who was given a wonderful gift—"

"—Let me guess. A starving Vizier gave him a really nice chessboard."

"Where'd you get that idea?" asked my grandfather. He eyeballed me like I was crazy. "This story's about a Greek king who saved a satyr. As a reward, he was given the power to turn things into gold. Anything he touched—boom— solid AU. *'Whatever you need,'* the Satyr told him, *'touch it and it will be yours: gleaming and golden.'*

"Anyways it only took this nincompoop of a king one day of celebrating until he accidentally touched his wife and daughter. After a second day, filled with mourning, he realized that any food or drink he touched would also turn into inedible gold. By the third day, starved and grieved, the greedy king started to wish he could just die and join his wife and daughter as a golden statue."

"I've heard the story of King Midas, Grandpa."

"Ha! So you have. I was just going to fib and say I made it up." His brow wrinkled in concentration as he stared deeper into his Game Boy.

A pause.

"So what's your point?"

Clearly distracted by his Tetris game, his eyes flashed up to mine, then back to his game. "My point…yes. The point is, um. One second."

I shifted in my seat.

"Uh, the point is, don't fill your life with shiny junk. Or else you might as well not be human yourself. You can lose yourself." He shut off the Game Boy and winked. "Yeah, that sounds like a pretty good point to make."

I didn't smile. "What if you feel like you can't keep from losing yourself? How do you remember who you are when everything is changing at…an *exponential* rate?"

My grandfather reached across the coffee table and pinched me hard in the elbow, with unclipped, old-man nails.

"Ow! What the heck?" He had slightly broken the skin of my arm and I could already see a small bruise begin to pool.

"Just remember that pinch, is all," he said. "Remember that you wear the skin of

Adam and bleed the blood of Eve. And no matter what evolves, no matter how much folks these days want to forget it, no matter how far out of this solar system they travel, they'll always be wearing the same hide on their backs. You'll always be who you are."

I sat back in my chair and rubbed my arm. Hating myself, I started to grin because I knew he was right. I took another sip of coffee, less anxious this time, and reminded myself that this was still just a science fiction story anyways. At least, it would be for another six months' time.

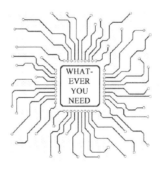

WHAT-
EVER
YOU
NEED

Someone Else's Job

I wanted to write one of those really amazing stories. The kind of story where you can feel little splinters of ideas circling you like voltaic ions as you write. The kind where light flushes through your head and sparks shoot out your fingers. Where the letters on your page crackle and pop and the spaces between each word hiss like the fuse of a time bomb. The kind of story where you dot an "i" and it bangs like a firework; the kind of story where you cross a "t" and can hear the hum of a serrated blade. I wanted to sit down on a whim and create something brilliant as a supernova. I wanted to play God. A god of my own little world. A god who looks down at a page of black squiggles and white line breaks and says, "It is good." I wanted to draft and design and finally, offer my meager two-dimensional creation as homage to the author of my genesis, and the genesis of one hundred and twenty-five billion galaxies.

The more I shaped and hatched and weaved and layered, the more I decided that my story should be mine alone. It was my world, after all. I fashioned it. What claim does anyone have to what is mine? It was my right to sit down and think things into being. My wish was permitted before I knew it had been made. I was made responsible for Creation.

Subconscious thoughts—deep, underpinning things—are the swiftest travelers. Swifter than the speed of sound (and the speed of silence, much faster). Swifter than the speed of light (and the speed of dark, much faster). Fast enough to fore-think themselves before the first layer of the first frontier of their very existence is conceived. Fast enough to leave retrogressive premonitions in their wake like comet-tails.

Thoughts arrive from nothingness and hurtle into somethingness. They shoot like lightning, faster than the speed of understanding: luminous things that begin to live and breathe before we realize we've thought them. Thoughts, once they contain Creation, are the most dangerous things that exist.

I didn't know how I became a creator anymore than I knew where my most inventive thoughts crystallized. I didn't realize how *in over my head* I truly was. I never considered that my very thoughts would be spoken into reality, beyond the world of a page, and into the physical dimension. Oftentimes, I found, before you know what is happening, before you can will your mind to dwell on excellent and praiseworthy things, it's deep parts may think terrible thoughts.

I killed my imagination as best I could before

too much damage was done on myself, my loved ones, and my universe. Not before some grotesque things took place. Everyone knows that once you think a thought, it can't be *un*-thought.

My left hand scribbles this letter. My right is now an angry red tentacle. My feet are bound into fleshy rollers fused to wheels that scrape and bleed whenever my bearings roll. A thin periscope juts from my left eye and stretches a meter above my head, making it impossible to drive a car or go out in public. When your imagination knows no limits, neither does your suffering.

I will control myself. I wasn't built to create in earnest. My mind is far too unstable a cocktail to do much more than think chaos into harmony. I wasn't made to do much more than play house on a black and white page. Create order out of chaos? That's someone Else's job.

I live on the Canadian cape now in a soundproofed, one-room apartment a few miles from Quebec's old quarter. It's me, four white walls and an unremarkable view of the Saint Lawrence river—always grey. I work from home as an accountant. I do not dare to think thoughts more vivid than the collection of data and the shuffling of numbers.

But occasionally, one of those shuffling numbers starts to dance. Then, before I can stop my mind from wandering, a number jumps off the page. Every once and awhile, a number begins to contort into a squiggle— something that resembles a living, breathing letter.

From time to time, the other numbers crawl off the page like corpses from a graveyard before I can keep myself from imagining. They twist and transmute into words and it's only a matter of time before they link arms and march united off the table towards me, an army of sentences, advancing onto my skin and over my body and into my mouth and inside my bloodstream as I try to *STOP THINKING* about the diverse, bizarre, malformed figures they've become…before it is too late.

Tower of Selfoss

One time, I built a skyscraper when I was in third grade. It was made of snow and it reached to the sky. I built it three months after my dad left us. In Iceland, during the winter months, nights were hard to get through if you didn't have electric heating. When the woodstove burnt low, you could get woken up late at night just by the sting of cold on your face. When I built the tower, I still remembered him fairly well—especially the details, like the feel of his stubble on my cheek when he would put me to bed. My dad visited my room each night when he got home from work, even after I was on the old side of childhood. Each time he arrived at my door, he always had the same snack: a glass of water, a square pat of butter and a slice of soft, homemade bread.

"Don't let your mum find the plate," he'd say with a wink.

Then he would sit and we would start to talk and before long, he always had me in stitches. He never made me say my prayers unless I wanted to, but sometimes I could see him scribbling discreetly on sticky notes while we talked. He snuck the notes into odd places of my room when he thought I wasn't looking—at the bottom of a dresser drawer or inside the pocket of a discarded pair of pants—and they always had Bible verses written on them. I thought perhaps that was his way of teaching me about God while still letting me make up my own mind about the Bible. That's what I still choose to think today. Every night without fail he did this, until one time, he didn't. Just like that, during my first week of third grade, he was gone.

I think my mum changed a lot after he left. For one, she bought me a cell phone and insisted that I carry it at all times so she would always know where I was, and so we could always communicate. That was about the only thing she ever insisted on. Whatever I wanted to do, no matter how stupid, she would just shrug her shoulders in a sort of defeated slump and remind me to keep my cell phone on me.

She said not to be angry, said that my dad had reasons to leave, good reasons, and that he was a good man. She said that he still loved me and that he was doing what was best for our family. I didn't understand what she meant and I never tried. I didn't want to wrap my head around her words, or how life would be with him gone.

Instead, I started to build things. Houses made of cards and castles made of toothpicks. One week, I even built a fortress of blocks that went up to the ceiling of my Sunday school classroom. I asked my teacher to place the final block snug between the tower and the ceiling and I stared at my tower for a minute, then kicked a sharp blow to the bottom block and watched the cardboard bricks tumble.

The Sunday school lesson that week was about the Tower of Babel. In was a story about a bunch of men who built the first skyscraper. I half-listened, while my Sunday school teacher flipped through a picture book and did his best to tell the story with a dramatic voice.

"They wanted to be the first men to build a tower so large, it would sit beside Heaven's gates," he said. "They thought if they lived in heaven, they would be like angels, or even gods. Their tower stretched up, up, up one hundred, five hundred, one thousand feet. The land below them must have looked like a brown and green blanket. The clouds must have drifted into their tower like cotton in the wind. The stars must have hung like pale jewels mere feet above their heads."

The teacher furrowed his brow and changed his voice to sound gravelly and dubious. "'This is it,' said the leader of the men. 'We must be close to heaven by now.'

"But before the leader could say another

word, lightning crackled through the sky. The men were close enough that the static charge made their faces itch. The lightning struck again, so loud that the men heard nothing for days, save for a distant ringing in their eardrums, no louder than a mosquito's whine.

"And just like that," finished my teacher, letting the last page of the picture book flip, "Everything was changed forever. Sound crept back into their ears, but each man's words sounded strange to the other. It was like listening to the mumbling sound people make when they talk in their sleep. Just as the builders closed in on Heaven, nothing would ever make sense again."

I thought about that story as I bundled up to play in the snow one morning. At that time of year in my village of Selfoss, the sun set at two o'clock in the afternoon, but there were still some hours of daylight left. My mum protested weakly as she dressed for work, but I told her I wanted to play while there was still some light. She shrugged her shoulders, bit her lip and nodded her head. She managed a smile later as she pulled out of the driveway in her waitress uniform; her hand rose slightly in a halfhearted goodbye as she drove away.

I picked up a shovel and began to toss the snow in my yard into a pile. My mittens were slippery against the plastic handle shovel and dampness seeped into my toes through my boots. Before long my entire yard was stripped of snow—just a hardened, naked lawn with a huge white lump in the middle.

I spent the rest of the morning scraping snow off of the driveway and heaving it onto my tower. It felt good to dig and shovel and toss everything on my yard into that lump, don't ask me why. My arms hurt and my legs were logs, but I didn't want to stop shoveling. So, I asked my neighbor, Mrs. Øveraasen, if I could shovel the snow from her lawn and use it for my tower. She looked at me with a sad smile, then nodded. Of course I could.

Trees in Iceland are sparser than hair on the head of a man in his eighties, but if I were to guess, I'd bet my tower was above tree line. I asked my neighbors the same question I asked Mrs. Øveraasen and they all nodded, some of them amused, others confused. Some offered to help me shovel but I said I'd rather dig alone. Only one person, Mr. Skarsgård, asked me why I was building up such a large mound of snow.

"Hoping to find something special up there?"

"I just like shoveling," I said. Shoveling made sense.

Soon I could see the entire city of Selfoss from the top of my tower. Over there was the bridge over the Ölfusá river; there the community geothermal pool. There, the Grimsborgir bed and breakfast; over there the steeple of Laugdælakirkja chapel—the very same place I'd heard that stupid story. I saw the giant hour-hand strike twelve on the belfry clock at village hall. It was hot above the city in the direct sunlight, but I still couldn't stop shoveling. My tower wasn't finished.

I sat and peered down at the street below me. It was windy, and I was too high up to make out the pavement cracks the frost had wedged into the road. My street was just a long strip of grey with a center line of dashes, like a row of the serrated writing paper my primary school teacher made us use to practice our cursive.

Joggers the size of toy army soldiers stopped below, staring up at me with hands above their brows, as if in salute to my creation. A few of them had their phones out and were taking pictures. When all my neighbors' lawns were empty, I fished my cell phone out of my snow pants. I was only supposed to use it to communicate during emergencies, but on a whim, I dialed zero, and pushed the green call button in the top left corner. I asked the operator to transfer me to the Selfoss Public Works department. The phone rang three, six, nine times, before the click of a receiver sounded.

"Selfoss Public Works Department, this is Runólf Nyström."

Mr. Nyström's voice was low and coarse. He sounded like he was bald and had a mustache. I asked him, a little nervously, if he would let me borrow a dump truck to haul extra snow from the city to my yard.

"I'm building a snow tower," I began. "And I've been shoveling all morning—"

———

To my amazement, Mr. Nyström stopped me mid-sentence. There was no need for me to explain.

"You're a boy who likes to shovel," he said. "Shoveling makes sense."

He said the town had more dump trucks than they needed and more snow than they knew what to do with since last week's blizzard. Before half an hour had passed, a line of dump trucks was positioned single-file in front of my house, each hauling a ton of dirty, off-white snow.

The sun sunk as my tower grew and at last, the giant mound of snow cast a shadow over the town like a looming ghost. I could see the southern edge of the country from the top of my tower. I saw city lights flicker to life like fireflies shivering in the winter air. I saw Hveragerði to the Northwest, and the southern harbor of Eyrarbakki, frothing pale in the sunset. The Norðurninn and Smáratorg skyscrapers in Reykjavik city were just below eye-level.

A cold gust of wind slinked across the back of my neck as the sun made contact with the horizon below. The sky was pink with tiny slivers of purple. I stopped only for a moment to take in the view (I no longer liked the way it felt to stay still or quiet for long) and then went back to shoveling.

Minutes, or hours or perhaps a different period of time later, my cell phone rang and I staked my shovel in the snow. I thought the call might be from Mr. Nyström, but instead I heard a voice that was almost a whisper.

"Honey?" my mother asked. The word sounded tentative, as if she were a scared child asking for a grownup to reassure her. "Have you been outside all day, just shoveling?"

"Yes," I answered. I pinned the phone between my shoulder and ear and patted the snow at the top of the tower, almost lovingly, into an even plane.

A second passed, then she told me she wished I would come down from whatever I built. She said I was scaring her.

"Please," her voice trembled. "Come in and I'll put a log in the woodstove. I'll make you a bowl of hot soup and put your snow pants in the dryer. Just come down from there, so we can talk."

I climbed a few steps downward then stopped. I wasn't ready to go back into that house. It was as if a layer of ice was expanding inside me when I thought about the hardened, naked yard, the too-cold house, the half-empty garage, even the idea of talking any longer with the confused woman so different from the mother who once cared for me. Those memories were just a jumble of confused, hurt chaos.

"I have to keep shoveling, mum." I said.

Pause.

A haze of static began to claim my cell phone's signal. I could only imagine her shoulders slumping. At last, amid the growing crackle I could just make out the words, "Then keep shoveling, honey, if that's what makes sense."

The sky phased to dark purple while I worked, then to black, like an inky bruise. My snow gear, once soggy, grew rigid, as the wetness in my clothing froze. I shivered and shoveled and thought about my dad and the tower of Babel and about how absurd it was for someone to ever believe you could get to Heaven, no matter how high you built. I thought about Sunday school, about kicking out the bottom block to my cardboard tower. I thought about God and why he had cracked his lightning on Babel like a whip just for the fun of wiping out reason and sense.

The stars winked into their assigned places. The air was thin and I had to pull in long gulps of air to fill my lungs. There was no sun in the sky to help me guess the time and each occasion that I needed to retrieve a shovelful of snow from ground-level, I had no idea how long it would take. I would have guessed it took me a week to climb down the first tier of my tower, a month to slide down the middle tier and a year to make the final stretch to my yard. At last, with blistered hands, I scooped my shovelhead under the last bump of snow.

This is it. I shook from fatigue and cold. *As close to Heaven as I'll ever get.*

I marched slowly upward—not because I was tired, but because I could start to guess what was at the top of my own Tower of Babel. I was too cold and wet to care about what would happen when I finished. Would lightning strike? Maybe I would go crazy and come down jabbering like a lunatic. I just kept stomping upwards with a shovelful of snow held in front of my chest.

I blinked when I reached the top. The continents were spread out below me— majestic, brown and peppered with swirls of white. There were Canada and America in front of me. Above me, more or less, was Greenland; below me, Europe and Africa. I squinted east in hopes of seeing the Great Wall of China—the long, razor-thin squiggle that reminded me of a tapeworm. I took a deep breath, jammed my eyes shut, and let the last of the snow slide from my shovel.

If lightning strikes, at least I'll know it's coming. At least I would know what to expect, which was more than I could say about the last three months of third grade.

Silence, then a sound. It wasn't deafening thunder. It sounded like two pins dropping one after another onto a crystal floor. It sounded like I had received a text message, but when I reached into my snow pants for the third time that day, I realized it was the sound of my phone battery dying. I started to shove it back into my pocket, but froze when I saw a yellow square stuck to my phone's back corner. It was a yellow sticky note and a Bible verse was written on it.

"What in the world?" I mumbled. My lips were numb and blue. The words had quotes around them and were scribbled in my father's handwriting. It hurt seeing that.

"Matthew 7:8-9," he'd written. "*For everyone who asks receives, the one who seeks finds, and to the one who knocks, the door will be opened. Which of you, if your son asks for bread, will give him a stone?*"

"Stop," I said. "Just stop." But a tear streamed from my face and my throat tightened. This was worse than lightning.

I didn't lose my mind and start talking nonsense after I read it. I just stood there, my chest hot and my eyes bleary. I wondered when my dad had slipped the note into my snow pants. Was it on the last night he saw me?

This was how God would punish me for

my tower. No lightning— just a parting stab from my father. He had told me once that God only punishes us in this life if we can learn something from it. If there was a lesson to be learned, it was lost on me.

Was it supposed to mean that God was okay with my skyscraper because I only built it to keep myself busy? A wishful thought crossed my mind and I hated myself for hoping.

Maybe—I thought—seeing the note meant that if I just kept asking, seeking, knocking, I wouldn't be disappointed. That after shoveling until my arms were raw, God would toss me a piece of bread and not a stone, at the end of the day. Could there be an answer and a father and a life if I just kept digging for it? It was a hopeful, pathetic thought, but when I looked down at the sticky note, the words seemed kind enough. But kind words just weren't God's style. Were they?

I looked back in the direction of Selfoss. I thought about the too-cold house below, the half-empty garage and the hardened, naked lawn. I lifted my foot to start the climb downward, then stopped and dropped my cell phone onto the snow. I'd finished shoveling, sure. But there was no way I could be finished asking, seeking and knocking. Unlike building a snow tower to the sky, those three things couldn't be done in just one day. I looked the other way, out to the North Atlantic Ocean.

For a second, a whiff of sea breeze made it through the cold air into my otherwise runny nose. I had only my snow pants, my shovel and a promise that my father was out there somewhere and that he loved me. I kicked my phone as hard as I could; watched it spin madly into the night. I could see it shimmering in it's descent for minutes. When it was out of sight, I dangled my legs over the top of my skyscraper and pointed them out towards the coast.

Ask, seek, knock, I reminded myself. I pushed forward and started to slide.

Sudoku and Reindeer Droppings

Nick was worn out. He was tired of being treated like he was too old to take care of himself; tired of being patronized and misrepresented; tired of his joint pain. Above all, he was tired of being *retired*.

Semi-retired, at least, he thought glumly.

He was in the home stretch of his double-shift. A sickly-saccharine odor wafted from the Yankee Candle Shop two stores down from his kiosk. He scratched his forehead between his eyebrows and watched Stanley, the Santa from zone four, cross the food court to the outlet bathrooms.

"Settling up for a long winter's piss," chuckled Stanley, in Nick's direction. Nick said nothing.

Nick's feet hurt from standing at his kiosk's North Pole façade for the last nine hours in the tightest buckled boots he'd ever worn. They were children's footwear, because the Billardtons Department Store could not afford to commission Santa boots his size. The old man rubbed his eyes and plastered on a smile— what his manager, Mr. Bradshaw called, the *magic-maker*. The magic-maker was a required facial expression to be worn at all times by the mall Santas in all seven zones of the department store—no exceptions.

Nick was a gnome of a man at barely five feet. He struck an odd sight, his great broken nose barely reaching above the mall sleigh and not an inch of fat clinging to his ribs. Many times when Nick wasn't present, Mr. Bradshaw had joked that Nick's height gave him an elfish appearance, which made him a good "Santa Candidate". He made sure not to mention this fact to Nick, although he would've loved to do so. However, HR policies being what they were, and his track record of pushing professional boundaries being what it was, he reserved his ridicule until after the old stooge was off-shift. He wasn't very fond of Nick—the man just wasn't the type of person he could like.

It could have been that Nick's beard was real and it was too long in Mr. Bradshaw's opinion. It could have been that Nick's speech occasionally trailed off into what sounded like some sort of inane rambling. At times, Nick also adopted an aire of ridiculous nobility, like he was some sort of chivalrous knight, and Mr. Bradshaw just *knew* this would make any child or parent visiting zone seven's branch of Santa's North Pole Village feel uncomfortable enough to squirm.

Yet, to Mr. Bradshaw's amazement, lines of children flocked across the mall, dragged their parents past all the other six North Pole stations, just to sit and talk to a grumpy senior citizen who put next to no effort into appearing jolly. What did Nick have that none of the other Santas had? It sure as hell wasn't the magic-maker.

Nick raised his bell, picked up the Naughty vs. Nice list Mr. Bradshaw had printed for him and, hating himself, recited his canned script.

"Ho, ho...HO! Merry Christmas! Happy holidays from the North Pole! Come have a seat. Ho…ho!" He clutched the pillow-belly strapped under his coat, feigning joy.

A headache was clustering behind his eyes. It was late-night on Christmas Eve. The night reeled in lots of business from procrastination-prone shoppers but the shift was somewhere between slow and dead at this hour when it came to kids. Dennis, the zone seven janitor smeared a cleaning solution across the tile floor and the acerbic chemical scent was seeping into Nick's nostrils. He felt lightheaded and a little nauseated. He clocked out for his evening fifteen-minute break and prepared for a rushed smoke in the parking lot. He stopped when a young girl wandered alone from the Waldenbooks outlet across the hall from his stand.

She was eight years old, but

something— perhaps it was her hair, or her clothes, or her eyes— made her look closer to twelve. Her skin was dark under her bottom lashes and her face was blotched red just above her cheekbones. She walked past a yellow "CAUTION: Wet Floor" sign and over to a heavily tinseled mall pillar. The girl leaned her small shoulder blades against the beam and looked unselfconsciously at the old man, as if she was too upset to care if he saw her staring.

Nick saw her, cursed in Greek and put his pipe and tobacco back underneath the sleigh. When he looked back at her a bit of his temper softened. Her head was cocked to one side and there was a distinct expression on her face. He'd seen the look on children's faces before, but it grew more and more rare each year. In the last five years that he'd worked as a mall Santa, he hadn't seen it once.

"Merry Christmas and happy, er..." He cleared his throat. "Happy holidays, sweetie. And, yeah. A happy new year as well."

She didn't roll her eyes, but it was clear that she wasn't in any spirit to hear

Christmas pleasantries. That was okay. Nick had no desire to dispense Christmas pleasantries.

"Hey, are your mother and father around?"

At this, her face scrunched up and a high sob (she tried to hold it back) hissed from her throat.

"Look, kid," he said, "Don't do that. I've got a headache and…please, no."

No change. He would have to think on his feet.

"You ever seen real magic—the kind that comes from the North Pole?"

He grabbed a chocolate coin from a golden box nearby and rolled it along his knuckles. As he caught it between the thumb and index finger of his right hand, the girl's eyes unscrunched, wet and blurry. Her vision sharpened just long enough to see the mall Santa blow on his hand and a chocolate coin vanish. The trick was a simple sleight of hand, but Nick was prepared to do better if there was a chance of keeping the whine of her sobs at bay. Nick hated whining and sobbing.

"That..." said the girl, forgetting to be

despondent for a moment, "that was amazing."

"Thank you."

"How did you do it?"

"Practice," he said. "Practice and perseverance. That trick took over a thousand and a half years for me to get down, truthfully. Had to persevere."

"Oh *sure*." The girl wiped her eyes and in spite of herself, started to smile.

"Really. My uncle— he was the bishop of Patara back then— taught it to me when I was about your age."

Nick didn't want to bring the girl to tears again by mentioning her parents, but he also didn't want her wandering around a mall alone at 10:45pm on Christmas Eve.

"You know, I have one last hour at my sleigh before I, uh, go back to the North Pole, or wherever. Will you help an old man finish a Sudoku puzzle while we wait for—um—while I finish out my last work shift of the season?"

"I've never played Sudoku," replied the girl.

"It's easy to learn," said Nick. "Yes, have a seat in the sleigh. I wish I'd had a game like this to keep me out of trouble when I was young. Unfortunately the monastery I lived in wasn't exactly stocked up on puzzles and board games."

"You got into trouble in a Monastery?" the girl asked.

"All kinds of trouble—I was neck deep in it, even after I grew up."

The girl appraised the tiny man in his red polyester suit. "I can't see you causing much trouble for anyone," she said.

The old Santa shrugged, but a mad glint shown in his eye. "Don't believe me? I'm an ex-convict, you know."

The girl's eyes widened into saucers. "You mean prison?"

Nick nodded. "Old jailbird that I am."

"For how long?"

"I served at least twenty years—after that, I either lost count or lost my wits."

The girl began to fidget and a question slipped from her lips before she could stifle it.

"Did you…hurt anyone?"

"Bah! Hurt nothing except the pride of a few Roman rulers. They slung me to the Big House for staying faithful to a

Nazarene King who changed and healed me. And by my beard, I'd do time for another *two hundred* years if they wanted to get tough and tell me who I can or can't pal with."

The old man was confusing. His bony shoulders were square next to hers as he talked. But even though he used strange words and didn't always make sense, he spoke to her like he would speak to a grown up. She liked that. He was careful to show that he took her seriously, even though she was very young. The girl climbed up into the sleigh as Nick pulled out his Sudoku booklet and applied his bifocals.

"I'm Zoe," she said quietly.

"That's a pretty name. It's a word from my native language, you know." The man didn't look completely up from the puzzle. "Means life in Greek."

"What's your name, Mister?"

The old man looked down his crooked spectacles at her for a long moment. The lenses sat awkwardly on his enormous, once-broken nose.

"Well this is Santa's North Pole Village, isn't it?" He seemed to be avoiding the question.

"Puh-leaze," said Zoe. "I know there's no such thing as Santa Claus. I'm not stupid. If he was real, he wouldn't be you. I don't think the real Santa Claus keeps calcium pills and Advil underneath his sleigh."

"Is that so?" the old man asked, growing indignant. "Well, since you've clearly lived long enough to come to that world-weary conclusion, then my name should make little difference to you. But for your information, I've worn many hats in my career and gone by many titles.
I've been called Papai Noel, San Nicola, Kaledu Senelis, the Saint of the Sea, Mikuláš, Sinterklaas, Shengden Laoren, Father Christmas, St. Nikolaus, Viejo Pascuero and Bishop Nicholas of Myra, for starters." Nick continued his ramble. "If it were any day other than Christmas Eve, I would say my name is "Mr." or "Sir" to a know-it-all like you. But, I suppose, because I am old and my bones are frail and because you can't even believe in someone sitting right beside you, you may as well just call me Nick."

Zoe was silent and felt sorry if she'd hurt Nick's feelings.

"I'm sorry...Sir," the title now seemed like the best thing to call him. "I didn't mean to sound like I don't believe you— nothing like that." She was careful to show that she took him seriously, even though he was very old.

"Well...then thank you. I had an inkling I saw the name Zoe at the bottom of my Nice List."

Ugh, he thought. *Any more talk like that and I'll make myself sick.*

"Wait," said Zoe, careful to remain polite. "At least admit the list isn't real. It's *laminated.* And it's even got a bar code in the bottom corner."

"True enough," laughed Nick, scribbling a six in the top right corner of his Sudoku booklet. "I stopped threatening to put kids on the Naughty List around 910AD. The whole thing was a bluff. What kind of Father Christmas would I be if I only gave rewards to people who earned them, eh? Even my manager, Mr. Bradshaw shows some undeserved kindness once and a while."

He's starting to ramble again, thought Zoe.

"For the record, I started out giving gifts to *anyone* in need—naughty, nice; virtuous or villainous. The stories must've started when someone caught me on a midnight charity run. All you need is one nosey-Joe to catch you sauntering around the neighborhood and tossing gold into the windows of poor houses. But I did try to be anonymous."

"So, if you're *Santa*—" Zoe scrunched quote-fingers in both hands as she said the words. "—And you actually do give handouts to everyone in the world, good and bad, how are you going to visit every family, when it's already..." She looked at her Hello Kitty watch, "...11:17 at night? You've got less than an hour."

The Santa beside her smiled. "How many Christmases can you remember, Zoe?"

"Seven so far. Does tonight count?"

"Yes. Well, I mean— no. Not yet. But pay close attention to tonight, because every Christmas Eve will count for something when you're looking back and remembering. Now. Think back to your earliest memory of Christmas Eve. Think of the gifts you may have waited for. Think of the excitement awaiting on Christmas day. Think of the ecstatic nervousness in the pit of your stomach when you prepared everything for a visit from someone you'd never seen."

Zoe wanted to say something fresh, but realized before long that her eyes, no longer sore and wet, had fluttered shut.

"Remember the tinsel and the bulbs, the bubble lights, the ornaments. Remember how carefully you arranged your Christmas tree. Remember the cookies and milk that you put out on your grandma's special plates— the ones with the blue flowers around the rim. Remember the time you snuck out of bed with hopes of seeing a man in a chimney, even if you did chicken out halfway to the living room because of your house's squeaky floorboards. Remember lying in bed, your heart pounding, wishing every second would pass faster, longing for Christmas. Do you remember?"

Zoe had no clue how the old man beside

her knew about her house's hardwoods or her grandmother's china plates, but she answered him without thinking.

"Yes. I remember." Her eyes opened and began to focus.

Nick nodded, satisfied. "Now, tell me child, did *time* behave the way it does every other day of the year?"

"No," she said. "Time kind of just...hung in the air."

"Suspended, like an ornament..." Nick trailed off, with something that sounded like nostalgia. "...as it has on Christmas Eve for the last two millennia, since the Creator of space and time came to Earth."

While a conversation and a game of Sudoku ran it's course between an old man and a young girl in zone seven of a Billardtons Department Store, Regina Kendall combed frenetically through zones two, three and four, retracing her steps in a manic search. Her lips were pursed and her eyes darted from side to side as if she was watching a secret pinball game. Her gate was short and tense, but her arms swung in a carefully casual manner— she was doing her best not to appear panicked— missing child or not.

Regina had more than one reason to be anxious. Christmas shopping aside, she'd searched six different department stores for the perfect Christmas outfit, with her boyfriend's daughter in tow. She chalked the trip up to quality time with Zoe, but apparently, the girl didn't see the outing that way. She had tried to make Zoe like her—it was bad business if her boyfriend's daughter didn't like her—but the girl was *impossible* to connect with. The girl was always in her room reading or writing or drawing. She was quiet, abnormally quiet, and Regina could hardly remember the last time Zoe had said more than a sentence to her. It was eerie. It gave Regina the creeps.

The one subject Zoe would talk about was her mother, David's ex-wife. Zoe went on about how much she loved her mom and how much David had loved her. She jabbered on and on about how her mother still loved her dad and how there were days when she thought he could still love her back. *Dream on, little imp.* David belonged to Regina now.

Regina wasn't sure if Zoe had any clue how much that kind of talk bothered her; she suspected that Zoe was reacting to her and David by trying to get under her skin. Regina's skin was thick indeed, but whenever she heard David and his soon-to-be ex-wife coordinating weekend custody over the phone, her blood began to boil. First the two had become civil, then cordial—even jovial now, and it made her angry. It wasn't right. If this was any indicator that her boyfriend was slipping away, this had to be due, at least in part, to Zoe.

The brat had better show up before David makes it to Billardtons, she thought, fuming. *At least I'll have some extra time to find her*: David was almost always a dunce when it came to matters of punctuality.

Losing David's child would not make matters any better between them. Her posture slackened as she searched, became less polished at the seams. After another twenty minutes, she took a large gulp of her pride—there was a lot to swallow—and rang a bell at the Customer Service counter. Almost immediately, a man with a clipboard and a thin, noose-tight tie appeared at the desk.

Punctuality, she mused, as she looked the man over. *That's nice, for a change.*

She squinted at his nametag. "Excuse me…Mr. Bradshaw."

"How can I help you, madam?"

She blushed slightly at being addressed as "madam", but maintained her focus. "I've lost my child and I need you to help me find her."

"So you grew up near an…a-*gore*-a?" Zoe rolled the word around in her mouth, making sure the emphasis stuck in the right place.

"You should have seen the pearls and

sapphires for sale there, or smelled the perfumes and the roasting lamb. Even to hear the sound of Greek port-merchants haggling is something truly special. In that marketplace, I once saved three good men from being executed."

"How did you do that?"

"Oh, a pinch of mischief. I just showed up in the executioner's dreams." A sly smile appeared under Nick's snowy beard. "I was a real pest to be honest. And I had a powerful appearance that convinced him his subjects were innocent after all.

"This was in *Myra*?"

"Yes indeed. And that miracle I told you about— the one where I multiplied all the wheat during that famine— that was in Patara. About twenty-five miles down the coast. Famines in those days were awful. The plagues were even worse."

Zoe nodded in solemn agreement. "Did you get sick?"

"I was one of the lucky ones. Some of my friend's weren't so lucky; my parents certainly weren't. And no amount of praying or fasting would make them better. That was one miracle the Lord wouldn't grant me."

Zoe felt her face start to scrunch again, but sitting next to her new friend, she felt braver than she'd felt in a long time. Brave as before her dad started dating again. Brave as before her parents started fighting.

"Sometimes I feel," she began, voice trembling, "like I lost my parents too."

Nick's pen halted on his booklet and he glanced up at the girl, then looked quickly back. He cleared his throat and seemed all of a sudden to be concentrating very hard on his last Sudoku corner.

"Maybe I stopped believing in you," Zoe said, "but I didn't stop for long."

Nick saw the look again on her face. The rare look.

"And maybe I didn't write you this year and I'm sorry about that."

Nick had been in his business long enough to guess what she would say next.

"Maybe I haven't even been good this year. But—and I know you're retired—if you have one miracle left in you, could you maybe pray or fast or something, that God will bring my family back together?

For a full minute the only sound to be

heard was a Celine Dion cover of "O Holy Night" through the store's hall speakers. At last Nick said, "I will pray."

David cracked three eggs on the edge of his stove and wondered if he was really hungry. He plopped them into a pan one by one and began to cook them sunny side up. He decided after a few minutes to flip them over easy. At last, he took a fork, scrambled them all about and shook some salt on top. He sat down and nibbled a few bites, then put down his fork and scraped the eggs into the garbage can. The blue-green letters on the microwave clock winked 11:00pm. He slumped in his seat.

He had a midnight date planned with his girlfriend. Regina had convinced him to go out to her place after Zoe was brought home and put to bed.

"Just pick out a proper gift for me,"

Regina had said, with a look of expectancy in her eye.

What did Regina expect from him? Perfume? Jewlery? A ring perhaps.

He didn't know why his last guess left him confused. After all, they'd been dating for almost a year. It made sense to get married, didn't it? The More David thought, the more he couldn't help but feel that a ring was what Regina wanted.

He ran his hand through his hair. There had not been this much guessing involved with Denise. They'd had their fair share of fights, especially for a pair of high school sweethearts who married young. But the most Denise would've expected from David on a night like tonight was a long kiss to close out the evening: unrushed and unplanned.

Denise. This was the first Christmas without her. The first Christmas that he wouldn't be staying up through the night, huddling and clasping, until at the first crack of sun they would creep to the living room to slip presents under their Christmas tree. Just a year later, those moments felt like they belonged to a different man.

But she's not a part of my life this year, he told himself. *It's better this way.*

The words sounded convincing enough in his mind, if not aloud. But shouldn't Denise be able to see Zoe, even after all that had happened? Was he really going to shut Denise out of their lives tonight? David didn't have time to think about that anymore. He didn't want to think about that anymore. He had to meet Regina and Zoe at the Billardtons Department store in twenty minutes and he would already be late. Regina hated it when he was late. He brushed crumbs from his shirt, patted some cologne on his neck and wrists and after making his way to the garage, jammed a key into his Subaru's ignition, backing himself out of the driveway.

The roads were dark and it was silent in his Subaru. It was harder to be dishonest with himself in the dark and silence. Finally, with a sigh that contained both resignation and relief, he pulled over to the road's shoulder and fished his cell phone out of his pocket. Flipping through his contacts, he reached the "D" section.

The name "Denise" was at the top of the list.

"What I don't understand," Zoe was saying, "is why after all those miracles you did and gifts you gave and sailors you helped and lives you saved and years you spent at the North Pole, you're okay with being retired. After all that!"

Nick's eyes made it clear that she'd struck another nerve.

"Well, what if I am retired?" cried the old Santa. "What if I don't fit in well enough to make a living anymore? What if I'm a washed up has-been whose life is behind him and who's better off forgotten?

"You know, when I started my campaign of charity, no one cared about the presents I gave. They cared about hope. And peace. And the truth, most of all. These days, most would pass up the only things that will make them happy for an X-Box or a plasma screen. I used to have three thousand employees who reported directly to me and they all say the same thing: that today people want too much. You know what?"

Zoe dared only to play as a willing recipient of his tirade. "What?"

"I'll tell you what. All three thousand of them were wrong. People these days are satisfied with too little. Modern souls are content with rotting junk. What's a plasma screen worth in the eternal long run, huh? And why, you ask, am I okay with being retired? Because nowadays, people don't want what I have to give."

"I'm...I didn't mean to..."

"No, don't apologize again," Nick rubbed his eyes. "I've had a long day, is all. And I've always had a short fuse. Just ask Arius of Alexandria what I did at the council of Nicaea. Losing my temper then," he clucked his tongue in a tut-tut, "not my finest moment."

"I bet," Zoe said in her most comforting voice, "that you must have at least had some exciting times when you worked at the center of the North Pole."

She thought for a moment that she saw

Nick's brow lift, saw a dim spark light in his eyes. Her grandfather had the same look when she asked him about his travels in Sicily during World War II. Yes, his stories bored her, but she knew that talking about his adventures made him happy and when she saw that look kindling in his eyes, she could tell that she'd hooked his spirits.

"You couldn't imagine the half of it," said Nick. "The pressure of making it to every home of the last three countries on my list: with only seventeen minutes left until Christmas day. The sight of Blitzen's hooves crackling against a canopy of storm clouds, scattering lightning below us. The sound of Donder's hind legs kicking thunder through the night sky. That was before pop singers ruined Christmas carols and advertisers marketed the holiday and everything to do with Christmas became packaged, plastic and sterile."

Zoe thought for a moment. Her eyes were tired now, but she felt as though there was something on the tip of her tongue that she needed to say.

"Nick?"

"Yes, Zoe?"

"I bet you're right with all that talk about people not wanting the best gifts you have for them. And I don't even see why all the pictures and drawings of you out there are…"

"Roly-poly? Elephantine? *Gelatinously endowed*?"

"Yeah," she said. She couldn't tell if he was making some kind of joke or just being wry.

"Well, I've fasted on Wednesdays and Fridays since the day I was born," said Nick. "Day-long fasts will thin you out quick. They have their benefits."

"But what about your charity?" Zoe asked. Was that worth it's while in the end, even if you never broke even on people who believed in your cause?"

"So you're starting to ask the same questions that I pose."

"Maybe I am. Then is there anyone on the nice list? Anyone who deserves hope?"

Nick pondered. "Well, there's Chahel and Pradeep in Mumbai. In Greater Copenhagen there's Astrid, who is worth my hassle. Kristoff in Oslo has a heart that's in the right place. And..."

"And?"

He sighed begrudgingly, "I suppose there's a girl in North America at a Billardtons Department Store who might deserve a bit of a break, if nothing else."

Zoe took the compliment in silence. "Then wouldn't you be happier if you weren't retired? If you were giving hope to everyone, whether or not they seemed to deserve it at first glance?"

Nick sniffed. He couldn't deny that Zoe brought up some good points. How old was she again— eight?

"You know, Zoe, you'd make a fine rhetorician, with some practice."

The words were indeed wise beyond her years, and they were starting to make Nick remember. He remembered the arctic breeze in his beard and the flecks of snow and ice in his hair. He remembered a hearty pipe in his mouth and the wind at his back. He even remembered old Rudolf, the German reindeer king who was bestowed the honor of lighting the Saint's way through the sleet and mist. Nick could still see in his mind's eye, the ancient lantern that hung from Rudolf's antlers just in front of his snout, a lantern that held the polar ember, a magic coal bright enough to rip through the black sky like a dagger through silk.

At last, he sat decisively up and began to hum a deep, strange tune in a deep, strange tongue. It was the Olden Song. The song that summoned beast and sleigh and put time under his command.

Mr. Bradshaw's night had

been exhausting. It was ten to midnight on Christmas Eve and Billardtons must have been the only department store in the entire U.S. that was still open at this hour. When the final t's were crossed and the last i's dotted, he guessed it would be closer to 1:30am.

Merry freakin' Christmas to me, he thought.

On top of everything he had dealt with that night, there was a raving woman by his side who had lost a child while she was trying a dress on. She'd been searching for the child for the last forty-five minutes. Still, things could be worse. At least she was a pretty, raving woman. The store's intercom-override had been out since black Friday and so here he was, peeking into the nooks and crannies of department store outlets, metallic gates pulled halfway to the floor.

Merry freakin' Christmas indeed.

"Have we searched all the zones?" Regina asked.

"As I said, we've searched six out of seven zones. I am confident your child must be in the seventh zone. I only wish you had notified us earlier, concerning your situation."

"Do you have surveillance tapes? Any security still staffing? I know you're able to call the police if necessary. Please, I am asking you, do not call them unless it becomes an ab-so-LUTE necessity. Oh, that would be such a disaster. If David ever—"

"Mrs. Kendall, please try to relax. I have this under control. We're going to find your daughter by hook or crook."

Regina inhaled through her nostrils and nodded. "*Kids*." She balled her hands into fists. "Good for absolutely *nothing*."

"Couldn't agree with you more," replied Mr. Bradshaw. He began walking and the pair resumed their search. "Except they're great for sales. The toy-related revenue we bring in this time of year, I'd swear the little snot-noses are the only thing keeping Billardtons out of the red." He cleared his throat. "Financially speaking, anyways."

A corner of Regina's mouth cracked. "I suppose everyone has their uses."

The lowered gate to zone seven of Billardtons could now be seen.

"I have to admit," Regina said. "I'm glad for your help. It's—*refreshing* to finally be around someone I can depend on to take charge of a situation or two."

Bradshaw puffed. "I didn't get promoted to assistant store manager without making an executive decision or two. Now just take a deep breath."

Regina obeyed him instantly, taking in a sharp and seemingly involuntary gasp. Two hallways down, a couple was entering the department store, talking like old friends.

One half of the pair was Regina's boyfriend. In an eye-blink, she found herself in a bewildered sprint towards the couple, with Mr. Bradshaw running confusedly behind her. But as Denise and David crossed the threshold of zone seven, Mr. Bradshaw and Ms. Kendall trailing close behind, the entire party beheld a chaotic sight.

Grunting and braying, stomping and making a mess of droppings on the nylon carpet of Santa's North Pole Village, were two rows of reindeer attached to an ornate sleigh that one would expect an Emperor to employ. Inside the sleigh stood Nick, humming a series of notes that were echoing and reverberating through the room. Standing by the sleigh, petting the lead reindeer, was a small girl.

"Nick!" yelled Mr. Bradshaw.

"David!" yelled Regina.

"Zoe!" yelled Denise.

"Dad!" and then, "Mom!" yelled Zoe.

Regina leapt like a singed cat at the sight of the live animals, and instinctively seized Mr. Bradshaw by the shoulder and bicep. *What muscles*, she thought, inspite of her panic. *He must be a gym-going man. Such discipline—so hard to find.*

Before long the humming had grown so loud that if anyone yelled anything else, it was not audible. The crystals, pearls and rubies that encrusted the exterior of the sleigh were growing more and more brilliant. They began to glow, then shine and then sear with light. Nick was sitting down in his sleigh now, testing the reins. During a mad moment of clarity within the thick chaos, Mr. Bradshaw thought he saw the old man mouth the word, "hope" to the girl standing nearby.

With a pop, a long hiss and a crack, the sleigh enveloped the room with light and when the department store manager dared to squint open his eyes, Nick's sleigh no longer rested on the soiled carpet.

What kind of a stunt was Nick pulling this time?

The old man was nowhere to be seen, nor did Mr. Bradshaw ever see him in a Billardtons Department Store again. Nick had swept the scene clear, leaving nothing but a smiling girl, two shaken parents holding hands, a filthy line of reindeer droppings, and a crumpled Sudoku booklet where the sleigh had been.

Acknowledgements

It seems I have to quote another author in this book—an author's whose life inspired me to read and whose death inspired me to write. His name is Ray Bradbury and he said, "You fail only if you stop writing." I decided recently to take his promise to the bank.

Some people spend years writing timidly, wondering if their voices are worth hearing; wondering if their ideas could ever be published. I've been encouraged to publish my writing by a number of writers and this is a modest entry.

"You fail only if you stop writing."

The words above are an encouragement—perhaps these thoughts will never make it from the scratched up surface of my kitchen table to the collection of stories in your hand, to the audio book in your ear, to the electronic page of your Amazon Kindle—perhaps they will linger abandoned in the in-between ether. But Ray says that no matter what, I still haven't failed; that my ideas are still worth something; that the simple phenomenon of a person's imagination in action is beautiful enough that it makes no difference how a book is received.

"You fail only if you stop writing."

These words are more than just an encouragement. They are fire-lit motivational. To write one's words and claim them as important is not enough—one must continue to write—otherwise one fails. With this in mind, I plan to publish more of these stories, these dreams on paper. I have in mind, as well, to say some thank you's.

Thank you, Ray Bradbury, for helping me to see the meaning of success. And thank you to Jane Yolen and Katherine Paterson for showing me that writers are not celebrities, but people too. Thank you to Brinda Charry, for giving me your honest opinion about parts of my writing that needed change and thank you to William Doreski, for spending four months helping me learn the true meaning of the word, "revise".

Thank you to Jane Yoga who had the firm kindness to show me what scholarly integrity means and thank you to Andrew Lantz, who told me to send off this work of playful fiction. Thank you to Bradley, my best friend, and to Scott, my brother. Above all, thank you to the sovereign Lord, Jesus Christ, who gave me the gift of creativity. I hope in the corners of my deepest places that I'll use Your gift in the right manner.

About the Author

Peter Best grew up in central New Hampshire and spent his childhood devouring both hot fudge Sundays and books by authors such as C.S. Lewis, Ray Bradbury, Orson Scott Card, J.R.R. Tolkien, Sir Arthur Conan Doyle and K.A. Applegate. He studied English, Education and Creative Writing at Keene State College.

Best is an avid traveler, musician and storyteller. He offers his vocal talents to Librovox.org and narrates the audio book adaptations of his written work. Currently he teaches English to children with special needs and daydreams about King Arthur.

He most recent books to date are titled, *Anyone Can Do It: Musings of a Neurotic Euro-Traveler* and *"S" is for Smokescreen.*

Kalia G!

You are a hilarious,
"Little-Mrs.-Sunshine" student!

I had to say thankyou for
working so hard at your
academics (no matter how you are
feeling).

This book is my way of
saying "thank you" for all your
hard work. — _____
(Mr. Best)

36069149R00078

Made in the USA
Lexington, KY
05 October 2014